# Little People, BIG DREAMS™
# J. R. R. TOLKIEN

Written by
Maria Isabel Sánchez Vegara

Illustrated by
Aaron Cushley

Frances Lincoln
Children's Books

John Ronald Reuel left South Africa when he was only three, excited to visit England and meet his grandparents. His father died soon after the family's departure, and he never went back to the land he once called home.

Ronald's mother taught him how to read and write.
He wondered where words and languages came from.

He also found great pleasure observing nature, and loved to draw majestic trees and stunning landscapes.

But when his family moved to the big city, Ronald felt nature had been taken away from him forever. At night, he dreamt of an imaginary world where magical flowers would grow on the graves of the brave.

Ronald spent long hours inventing secret languages.
He named the first of them Naffarin and loved repeating
its words. But he didn't just look for beauty in its sound;
he also gave each word a meaning.

After his mother died, he and his brother were left to the care of a friend, Father Francis, who gave them the best education. At King Edward's School, Ronald met three extraordinary boys: Rob, Geoffrey, and Christopher.

They were not just friends, but the members of a secret society that met every afternoon to read poems and stories. It was in one of these meetings that Ronald decided to learn everything he could about the origins of language.

He was studying English at Oxford thanks to a scholarship when the war started. One by one, he and his friends were sent to fight. When the war was over, only Ronald and Christopher were left to talk about it.

Ronald married his lifelong love, Edith. They had four children for whom he wrote magical stories. One evening, he read them the tale of a hero that looked like no other: a Hobbit.

It wasn't just his family who loved that story!
When *The Hobbit* was published, it became such a success
that everyone wanted more. The publisher urged Ronald
to write a second book, and he started immediately.

It took him twelve years to complete the 9,250 pages of *The Lord of the Rings*. A heroic tale where hobbits, dwarves, elves, wizards, and men joined together as friends to save Ronald's imaginary land: Middle-earth.

The book was so long that it had to be published in three parts, but his readers devoured them all. They were taken to an extraordinary world full of great legends, where the most ordinary of us could become a hero.

Ronald's vast world kept growing in his mind and on the pages of another book, *The Silmarillion*. It was a book that could never be completed, because the end of a story was always the beginning of a new one.

Little John Ronald Reuel—the king of modern fantasy—
kept writing day after day, and he loved every single moment
of it. Because he knew that it doesn't matter where we go,
what matters is that we enjoy the journey.

# J. R. R. TOLKIEN

(Born 1892 – Died 1973)

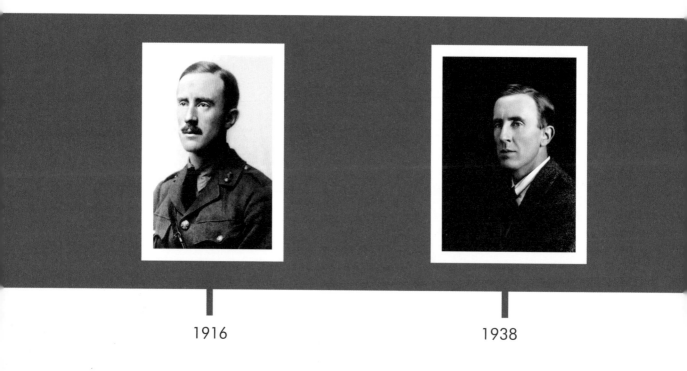

1916                                1938

John Ronald Reuel Tolkien was born on 3rd January 1892 in Bloemfontein, South Africa. Upon the death of his father when he was aged three, the family relocated to Birmingham, England. Mabel, his mother, encouraged his love of nature and began teaching him Latin. But when she died in 1904, Father Francis Xavier Morgan, a Catholic priest, became the guardian of Ronald and his brother. After graduating from Oxford University with an English Literature degree in 1915, Ronald immediately joined the army during World War One. He fought in the Battle of the Somme, in which two of his childhood friends were killed. In 1916, Ronald married Edith and together they had four children. To entertain them, he created fun, fantastical stories, and from these tales, *The Hobbit* was

1955

1970

created and published in 1937. A keen painter, he made intricate maps to bring the world of Middle-earth to life. He also created a whole new language for his characters, called Elvish. Ronald worked as a code-breaker for Britain during World War Two, but continued to build his fantasy world. He spent 17 years writing *The Lord of the Rings*, which saw elves, wizards, and men join together to fight evil. The story was so long, it was split into three books: *The Fellowship of the Ring*, *The Two Towers,* and *The Return of the King*. It became a best-seller and to this day, is loved by millions of fans worldwide. Regarded as one of the founding fathers of modern fantasy literature, J.R.R. Tolkien taught us about the power of the imagination, the beauty of language, and the strength of friendship.

Want to find out more about **J.R.R. Tolkien?**

Have a read of this great book:

*Who Was J. R. R. Tolkien?* by Pamela Pollack

Brimming with creative inspiration, how-to projects, and useful information to enrich your everyday life, quarto.com is a favorite destination for those pursuing their interests and passions.

Text © 2022 Maria Isabel Sánchez Vegara. Illustrations © 2022 Aaron Cushley.

Original concept of the series by Maria Isabel Sánchez Vegara, published by Alba Editorial, SLU.

Little People Big Dreams and Pequeña&Grande are registered trademarks of Alba Editorial, SLU for books, publications and e-books. Produced under licence from Alba Editorial, SLU

First Published in the USA in 2022 by Frances Lincoln Children's Books, an imprint of The Quarto Group.

Quarto Boston North Shore, 100 Cummings Center, Suite 265D, Beverly, MA 01915, USA

Tel: +1 978-282-9590, Fax: +1 978-283-2742 **www.Quarto.com**

A catalogue record for this book is available from the British Library.

ISBN 978-0-7112-5787-0

Set in Futura BT.

Published by Katie Cotton • Designed by Sasha Moxon

Edited by Lucy Menzies • Production by Nikki Ingram

Editorial Assistance from Rachel Robinson

Manufactured in Guangdong, China CC052022

3 5 7 9 8 6 4 2

Photographic acknowledgements (pages 28-29, from left to right): 1. 1916–, GREAT BRITAIN: The celebrated british Fantasy writer J.R.R. TOLKIEN (John Ronald Reuel, 1892-1973), author of book THE LORD OF THE RINGS, Unknown photographer during the WWI © ARCHIVO GBB via Alamy Stock Photo 2. Portrait of the English writer, John Ronald Reuel Tolkien (1892-1973), c. 1938 © IanDagnall Computing via Alamy Stock Photo 3. 2nd December 1955: John Ronald Reuel Tolkien (1892 - 1973) the South African-born philologist and author of 'The Hobbit' and 'The Lord Of The Rings'. © Haywood Magee/Stringer via Getty Images 4. Novelist and professor J.R.R. Tolkien sits against a tree. He was the author of The Lord of the Rings and The Hobbit. © Bettmann via Getty Images

# Collect the Little People, BIG DREAMS™ series:

FRIDA KAHLO · COCO CHANEL · MAYA ANGELOU · AMELIA EARHART · AGATHA CHRISTIE · MARIE CURIE · ROSA PARKS · AUDREY HEPBURN

EMMELINE PANKHURST · ELLA FITZGERALD · ADA LOVELACE · JANE AUSTEN · GEORGIA O'KEEFFE · HARRIET TUBMAN · ANNE FRANK · MOTHER TERESA

JOSEPHINE BAKER · L. M. MONTGOMERY · JANE GOODALL · SIMONE DE BEAUVOIR · MUHAMMAD ALI · STEPHEN HAWKING · MARIA MONTESSORI · VIVIENNE WESTWOOD

MAHATMA GANDHI · DAVID BOWIE · WILMA RUDOLPH · DOLLY PARTON · BRUCE LEE · RUDOLF NUREYEV · ZAHA HADID · MARY SHELLEY

MARTIN LUTHER KING JR. · DAVID ATTENBOROUGH · ASTRID LINDGREN · EVONNE GOOLAGONG · BOB DYLAN · ALAN TURING · BILLIE JEAN KING · GRETA THUNBERG

JESSE OWENS · JEAN-MICHEL BASQUIAT · ARETHA FRANKLIN · CORAZON AQUINO · PELÉ · ERNEST SHACKLETON · STEVE JOBS · AYRTON SENNA

LOUISE BOURGEOIS · ELTON JOHN · JOHN LENNON · PRINCE · CHARLES DARWIN · CAPTAIN TOM MOORE · HANS CHRISTIAN ANDERSEN · STEVIE WONDER

MEGAN RAPINOE

MARY ANNING

MALALA YOUSAFZAI

ANDY WARHOL

RUPAUL

MICHELLE OBAMA

MINDY KALING

IRIS APFEL

ROSALIND FRANKLIN

RUTH BADER GINSBURG

MARILYN MONROE

KAMALA HARRIS

ALBERT EINSTEIN

CHARLES DICKENS

YOKO ONO

MICHAEL JORDAN

NELSON MANDELA

PABLO PICASSO

AMANDA GORMAN

GLORIA STEINEM

FLORENCE
NIGHTINGALE

HARRY HOUDINI

J.R.R. TOLKIEN

ELVIS PRESLEY

NEIL ARMSTRONG

ALEXANDER VON
HUMBOLDT

NIKOLA TESLA

WILMA MANKILLER

## ACTIVITY BOOKS

STICKER ACTIVITY
BOOK

COLORING
BOOK

LITTLE ME, BIG
DREAMS JOURNAL

Discover more about the series at www.littlepeoplebigdreams.com